Old MacDonald had a Zoo

CP/494

OLD MACDONALD WINS LOTTERY

An elderly farmer has won one million gold coins on the lottery. Mr Old MacDonald, of MacDonald's Farm, said: "I just need to find the right thing to spend it on now!"

ZOO FOR SALE

The City Zoo has come up for sale. Buyers should be aware that the zoo is in need of safety improvements, including electric fences and dinosaur-strength tranquilisers. The asking price is one million gold coins, a bargain for any animal lover.

ZOOKEEPER MISSING

Local zookeeper, Mr Arthur Kipper is missing. His boots were found in the penguin pool, his torn trousers in the lion cage and his hat and shirt in the monkey enclosure.

Spot the Bull and win one gold coin!

For Tom - Ooo! Ooo!
C.J. xxxxx

For Curtis, with love
T.M.

EGMONT
We bring stories to life

First published in Great Britain 2014
by Egmont UK Limited
The Yellow Building, 1 Nicholas Road,
London W11 4AN
www.egmont.co.uk

Text copyright © Curtis Jobling 2014
Illustrations copyright © Tom McLaughlin 2014
Curtis Jobling and Tom McLaughlin
have asserted their moral rights.

ISBN 978 1 4052 6712 0 (Paperback)
ISBN 978 1 7803 1492 1 (Ebook)

A CIP catalogue record for this title
is available from the British Library.

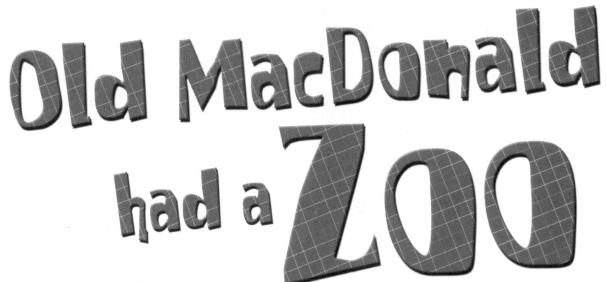

Old MacDonald had a Zoo

Curtis Jobling & Tom McLaughlin

EGMONT

Gift Shop

EXIT

Old MacDonald had a zoo,
ee-i-ee-i-oh!

Old MacDonald had a zoo,
ee-i-ee-i-oh!

And in that zoo he had some **penguins**,
ee-i-ee-i-oh!
With a **HONK HONK** here
and a **HONK HONK** there,

And in that zoo
he had a snake,
ee-i-ee-i-oh!
With a **HISS HISS** here ... and a **HISS HISS** there,
here a **HISS**,
there a **HISS**,

everywhere a **HISS HISS.**

Old MacDonald had a zoo,
ee-i-ee-i-oh!

And in that zoo
he had some **wolves**,
ee-i-ee-i-oh!

With a **HOWL HOWL** here
and a **HOWL HOWL** there,
here a **HOWL**, there a **HOWL**,

everywhere a
HOWL HOWL.

Old MacDonald
had a zoo,
ee-i-ee-i-oh!

And in that zoo he had some crocodiles,
ee-i-ee-i-oh!
With a **SNAP SNAP** here
and a **SNAP SNAP** there,

here a **SNAP**,
there a **SNAP**,
everywhere a
SNAP SNAP.

Old MacDonald had a zoo,
ee-i-ee-i-oh!

And in that zoo he had some vultures

ee-i-ee-i-oh!

with a **KAW KAW** here
and a **KAW KAW** there
here a **KAW**, there a KAW,
everywhere a **KAW KAW**

Old MacDonald had a zoo, **ee-i-ee-i-oh!**

And in that zoo he had a lion,
ee-i-ee-i-oh!

And in that zoo he had an elephant, **ee-i-ee-i-oh!**

With a **STOMP STOMP** here

and a **STOMP STOMP** there,

here a **STOMP,**
there a **STOMP,**

Gift
Shop

everywhere a
**STOMP
STOMP.**

Old MacDonald had a . . .